Dear Parent:

Your child's love of reading starts here!

Every child learns to read in a different way and at his or her own speed. Some go back and forth between reading levels and read favorite books again and again. Others read through each level in order. You can help your young reader improve and become more confident by encouraging his or her own interests and abilities. From books your child reads with you to the first books he or she reads alone, there are I Can Read Books for every stage of reading:

SHARED READING
Basic language, word repetition, and whimsical illustrations, ideal for sharing with your emergent reader

BEGINNING READING
Short sentences, familiar words, and simple concepts for children eager to read on their own

READING WITH HELP
Engaging stories, longer sentences, and language play for developing readers

READING ALONE
Complex plots, challenging vocabulary, and high-interest topics for the independent reader

I Can Read Books have introduced children to the joy of reading since 1957. Featuring award-winning authors and illustrators and a fabulous cast of beloved characters, I Can Read Books set the standard for beginning readers.

A lifetime of discovery begins with the magical words "I Can Read!"

Visit www.icanread.com for information on enriching your child's reading experience.

*To Eugene—there's no
friend like an old friend
—B.H.*

*For my wife, Lorien
—G.F.*

I Can Read® and I Can Read Book® are trademarks of HarperCollins Publishers.

Clark the Shark: Friends Forever
Copyright © 2022 by HarperCollins Publishers
All rights reserved. Printed in the United States of America.
No part of this book may be used or reproduced in any manner whatsoever without written permission except
in the case of brief quotations embodied in critical articles and reviews. For information address HarperCollins Children's Books, a division of HarperCollins Publishers, 195 Broadway, New York, NY 10007.
www.icanread.com

Library of Congress Control Number: 2021943712
ISBN 978-0-06-291259-6 (trade bdg.)—ISBN 978-0-06-291258-9 (pbk.)

Book design by Chrisila Maida

22 23 24 25 26 LSCC 10 9 8 7 6 5 4 3 2 1   ❖   First Edition

I Can Read!

READING 2 WITH HELP

CLARK THE SHARK
FRIENDS FOREVER

WRITTEN BY BRUCE HALE   **PICTU**

HARPER

An Imprint of HarperColli

Clark the Shark was excited.

"Look, it's a contest!" he said.

"The winner gets a bunch

of Captain Suckermouth comics,

signed by Captain Suckermouth!

our help to win."

But Joey Mackerel had problems
of his own.

"I lost my—" he began.

"Never mind that," said Clark.
"You've got to help me draw
a cartoon to enter the contest."

5

"But I—" Joey began.

"Where are your crayons?"

asked Clark.

Joey frowned.

"You never listen.

I'm not in the mood.

Just go away!"

Clark swam off.

"What's wrong with Joey?"
he wondered.

Clark tried to draw

the cartoon by himself.

It was less than perfect.

"I need help!" he said.

"Why not ask Joey?" said his mother.

"I can't," said Clark.

"Joey told me to go away,

but I didn't do anything wrong."

He told his mom what happened.

"It sounds like Joey was upset,"
said Clark's mother.

"Did you ask him why?"

"No," said Clark.

"Did you listen to his problem?"

"No," said Clark.

"I think Joey needs a friend,"
said Clark's mother.

"A friend who can listen."

11

Clark wanted to be a good friend.

He wanted to help Joey

and also win the contest.

But Joey didn't want to see him.

What to do?

When he peeked in the window
of Joey's house,
Clark saw another friend
comforting him: Amanda Eelwiggle.

"Why is Joey so upset?"
Clark asked Amanda
when she came outside.
"Does he hate me?"
"His pet catfish died,"
said Amanda.

14

"You'd know that if you weren't so focused on your silly contest," she told Clark.

"Friends put friends first."

"Do you think playing reef ball
would cheer up Joey?"
Clark asked.
"Would that cheer you up
if you lost Lulu?"
Amanda asked.

Back home, Clark looked at his pet.

He would feel sad if he lost Lulu.

Joey must be pretty sad too.

Clark sighed.

It was hard work being a good friend.

You had to listen.

You had to put your friend first.

You had to do all kinds of stuff.

How could he ever remember it all?

Then Clark got a sharky idea.

Maybe a rhyme

would help him remember?

He thought and thought,

and thought some more,

until he came up with this . . .

"If you want to be a friend,
be a true one, don't pretend.

"Listen closely, treat them kind,

be there for them, rain or shine.

"Stick with them until the end,

that's the way to be a friend!"

said Clark.

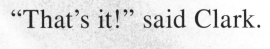

"That's it!" said Clark.

"A real friend would try

to cheer up Joey."

But how?

Maybe a sympathy card would help?

Even though Clark couldn't draw,

he sat down and tried his best.

Clark went to Joey's house,
but he was afraid to talk to him.
What if Joey was still mad?

So Clark folded his card
into a paper airplane
and sailed it through Joey's window.

When Joey read the card,

he cracked up so hard!

"This is the worst drawing,

but the best wishes," he said.

"Thanks, Clark!"

Clark was so relieved.

He asked how Joey was doing.

Joey talked.

And Clark listened.

Then Joey had a great idea.

"Let's do a catfish cartoon

for the contest," he said.

"Brilliant!" said Clark.

So that's what they did.

And when they sent it in . . .

Clark and Joey won first prize!

They celebrated

and shared all the comic books.

Friends to the end!